Patricia Polacco

John Philip Duck

Philomel Books

In loving memory of Robert McCloskey, inspiration to me since I was a child.

Edward was a sweet boy who lived with his family on a small farm just outside Memphis in the foothills of Tennessee. Times were hard. There was a depression on and money was hard to come by. Even though Edward was just a lad, he and his father worked at the same hotel in Memphis. During the work week they stayed at the hotel, but on the weekends they both went home.

Edward loved the weekends. He and his family all gathered around the old radio in the parlor and listened to grand music. Edward especially loved hearing the brass bands play marches by John Philip Sousa! It made Edward dream about wearing a snappy uniform with shiny brass buttons. "Someday I'm going to have a uniform just like that! You'll see!" he'd say as he marched around the parlor to the lively music.

Edward was a dreamer, all right. One time, right in the middle of chores
there on the farm, he stopped and looked up in wonder. Wild ducks were
calling and were flying in perfect formation. "Ain't they grand, Pa? Look how
they fly in perfect V's, and look, they're follering a leader. See, the one right in
the point on the V." He secretly wished he could be with them, "just to touch
them feathers and look at them real close-like."

One weekend, while Edward was doing his chores, he heard a tiny little sound coming from some bullrushes on the edge of the pond. When he looked, there it was! The tiniest, scrawniest little duckling he had ever seen. A wild one, left shivering from the cold. Edward scooped it up in his hands. He couldn't see its mother anywhere! He slipped it into his shirt so it could be next to his warm skin.

That night at dinner, Edward got the duckling to eat right out of his hand.

"Usually when they are this little, they don't survive," Edward's ma said.

"If I can make this little critter well, can I keep him, Ma?" Edward pleaded.

"This little creature will take constant care, and what will he do while you are gone all week at the hotel?" Pa said.

Edward thought for a moment. "Can't we take him with us, Pa?"

"To the hotel?" His father scowled.

"Please, Pa . . . I'll keep him in a box in the pantry right next to the cook-stove so he'll be warm. Big Joe will let me, I know he will," Edward begged.

"Big Joe is only the cook. I'm worried about Mr. Schutt!" Pa said. Mr. Schutt was the hotel manager.

But then his pa and ma looked at each other. They could see how much Edward wanted this duck. "Well, I guess we can give it a try, but you have to keep him hidden or we could both lose our jobs!" Pa warned.

Now, Frank Schutt was a huge man. He was the general manager of the hotel. He ran a tight ship, and his word was law! His booming voice echoed down the hallways as he inspected his staff. But he was always fair.

Edward sneaked his little duckling into the pantry next to the stove, where he and Big Joe, the cook, could look after him.

Of course, after a time all of the hotel staff came into the kitchen just to see how the little fella was doing. Everyone swore to keep the little duck a secret from Mr. Schutt.

Although Edward took him home on the weekends, the duckling soon became a fixture in the kitchen. Pretty soon he could hop out of his box. Then he ventured into the halls.

But one day, the little duck waddled right into the lobby. Mr. Schutt almost saw him, but Edward grabbed up the little fellow and stuck him into his shirt.

"You there, my boy," Mr. Schutt bellowed. "Mr. Templeton in 203 wants his shoes shined. Now, you run up and put a shine in 'em like a mirror."

About then the little duckling gave a very loud quack.

Mr. Schutt narrowed his eyes and came right up to Edward. "What was that?" he barked.

One of the bellmen started to cough loudly. "That was me, sir. My pardon, sir."

Mr. Schutt glowered at him for a moment. "Well, take care, Bingham . . . take care!" he called out as he harrumphed away.

After that close call, everyone who worked at the hotel took turns keeping the little duckling out of Mr. Schutt's way. It was their secret!

Whenever Edward was busy, they all helped hide the little duck.

Chef Voulliard hid him under an entrée lid.

The manicurist carried him on her cart.

The valet kept him under his hat.

The front desk crew kept him in a vacant key box.
The doorman kept him in his pocket.
Everyone fell in love with that little duck.

One night, after Mr. Schutt had left for the day, Edward put a John Philip Sousa march on the phonograph.

"Watch," Edward said to the staff. "All I have to do is tap this stick on the floor and he'll do what I taught him to do." Edward tapped twice and the little duck turned around and around.

Three taps and the little duck marched up and down the lobby hall.

Four taps and the little duck stood as still as a statue.

Edward tapped out a pattern and the little duck hopped right into the lobby fountain. He did one or two tricks right there as Edward tapped his stick. Then he tapped again and the little duck hopped out of the fountain and down the hall.

"Amazing!" everyone exclaimed.

"He marches as proper as John Philip Sousa himself," someone said.

Edward stopped. "That's it! That'll be his name: John Philip Duck." Everyone laughed.

One day not long after, some of Mr. Schutt's hunting buddies were staying at the hotel. They were in town to duck hunt at the crack of dawn the next morning. As a joke, they put their live duck decoys into the lobby fountain pool.

Edward watched them swimming there and his heart ached at the thought of what they would be used for.

"Come on, boys!" Mr. Schutt's voice boomed. "Let's git to the kitchen and pack some provisions for your hunt tomorrow."

Edward's heart stopped. John Philip Duck was in the kitchen! Big Joe must have heard Mr. Schutt, because Edward saw him slip John Philip into the fountain with the other ducks.

"He'll never find him there!" Big Joe whispered as he passed Edward.

All that evening, every time Edward tried to get John Philip out of the fountain, Mr. Schutt seemed to be there with his hunting buddies.

Then, to Edward's horror, the men started pulling the ducks from the fountain and putting them in cages to take for the early morning hunt.

Edward felt his heart skip a beat as he watched the hunters stuff John Philip into a cage. Edward HAD to do something! "Wait, please!" he finally called out. "One of them ducks is my pet!"

Mr. Schutt and his friends stopped and turned. Mr. Schutt glowered at Edward. "Well, boy, what is he doing here in my hotel, and in my fountain!" he bellowed.

Edward almost started to cry. He told the red-faced manager the whole story of how John Philip came to be at the hotel. Mr. Schutt's eyes softened.

"Please, sir. Let me show you the tricks that John Philip can do!" Edward pleaded as he took his duck out of the cage.

"All right, boy, let's see!" Mr. Schutt barked as he and his friends took seats nearby to watch.

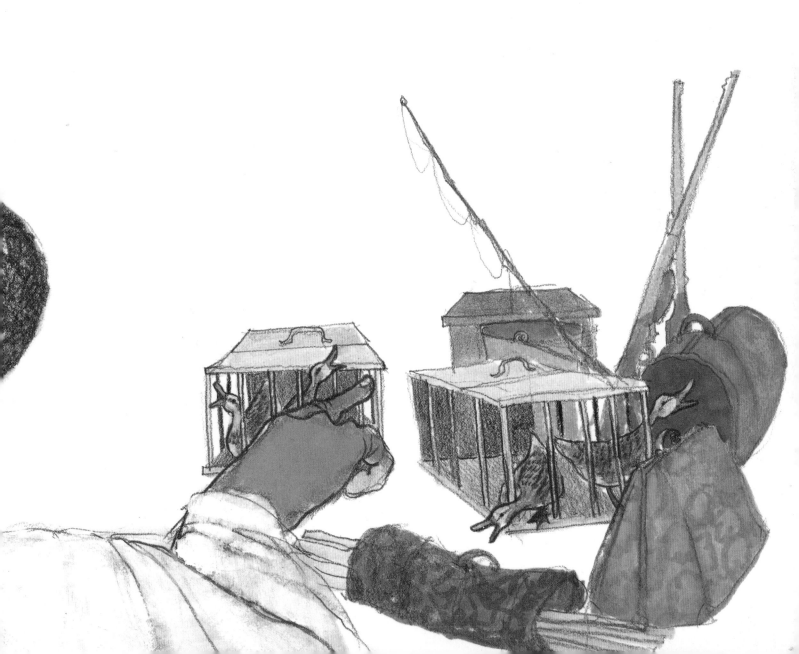

Edward turned on the music. It was a Sousa march, and John Philip was in the best form he had ever been. He did all of his tricks without a hitch. He marched to and from the fountain. He hopped in and out of the fountain pool on command, just as Edward had taught him.

When John Philip was done, he waddled up to Mr. Schutt and cocked his head.

"Well, I never did see!" Mr. Schutt said almost in a whisper.

One of the hotel guests had seen it all and commented to Mr. Schutt, "What an unusual touch."

A well-dressed lady cooed, "I've never seen, in all of my world travel, a hotel with live ducks swimming in the lobby fountain! Wonderful, simply wonderful!"

"All of the guests enjoyed John Philip, sir," one of the bellmen exclaimed.

"Oh, sir," Edward said. "Wouldn't it be something if we could have ducks swimming in the fountain all the time!"

Everyone cheered their approval.

"Mr. Schutt, I could teach all of them very ducks to do tricks and march in and out of the fountain." He pointed to the hunters' ducks. "People from everywhere would come and see them. I know they would!" Edward blurted out.

Mr. Schutt thought for a very long time. He conferred with his hunting pals. "Tell you what, boy. We're gonna give you all of these ducks here to train up. I'm giving you a month to train them all to march into the lobby, git in the fountain and stay there all day, then march out again."

"And can John Philip stay here, too, except for when I take him home, that is?" Edward asked hopefully.

"Well, I guess he can," Mr. Schutt said as he marched away. "But you have one month!" he bellowed as he disappeared around the corner.

Mr. Schutt let Edward build a duck house up on the roof of the hotel. Every day Edward trained the ducks to march to the tapping of his stick. He got them to march from the roof, down the hall and even into the elevator. Down twelve floors it went. When the doors opened, the ducks marched into the lobby. At first they all scattered, but John Philip helped Edward round them up.

Finally Edward got them all to march to the fountain, go up three steps that he had made, and plop into the water.

But they hopped out and waddled around the lobby again!

Edward worked and worked with them for days. At last he got them trained to stay in the fountain all day. In good time too, because his month was up the very next day!

It was a Friday afternoon at three. Mr. Schutt and many hotel guests were already seated in the lobby, waiting. Edward was very nervous. He took the elevator up to the roof to get the ducks. John Philip led them all down as usual. They marched into the elevator as usual. Those twelve floors seemed to take forever. When the doors opened to the lobby, Edward could see Mr. Schutt. He looked stern.

Edward then noticed that the bellmen had rolled out a red carpet to the fountain. They had placed velvet ropes on either side of the carpet. All of the staff winked at him. Then Edward heard a brass band playing a John Philip Sousa march! His own pa had put on the record. He looked so proud, but a little worried too.

Edward tapped his stick and all the ducks marched perfectly down the red carpet. People *ooohed* and *awwwed* as they passed by. With a few taps of his stick, the ducks hopped into the fountain, one by one. The carpet was rolled up, the velvet ropes and stairs removed. The ducks swam and swam as people crowded around just to see them.

"Well . . . this, by dippie, is the best show I ever did see!" Mr. Schutt chuckled.

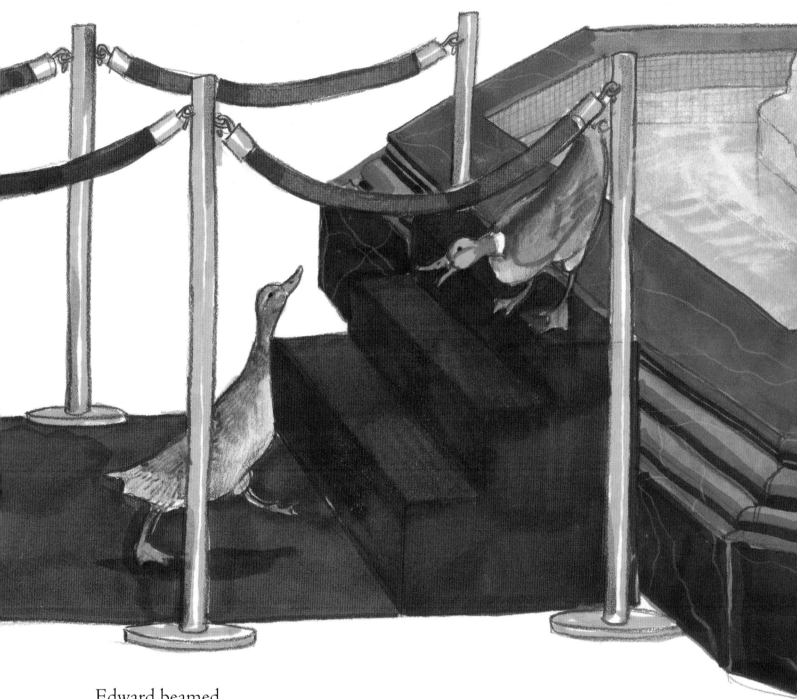

Edward beamed.

"But the test ain't over yet," Mr. Schutt added. "These ducks have to stay in this fountain all day!"

Edward knew that would be the biggest test.

All that day, he stayed out of sight and watched to see if any of his "trainees" tried to get out of the fountain. None of them did! They swam there all day long.

Then, at five o'clock, the red carpet was rolled out again. The velvet ropes and the steps put in place. The elevator opened. Edward tapped his stick and the ducks jumped out of the fountain, one by one. They marched up the red carpet again to a John Philip Sousa march, then waddled into the elevator, rode up to the roof and marched into their duck house.

"We did it!" Edward whispered to all of the ducks as he fed them their favorite mash. John Philip quacked loudly as if he were proud too. "None of this would have happened if I hadn't found you," Edward said softly as he petted John Philip's head.

Edward took the elevator downstairs again, and when the doors opened, Mr. Schutt was waiting for him. All of the staff was gathered there in the lobby with him. Edward's pa too.

Mr. Schutt cleared his throat. "We found this here uniform especially for you, my boy. You did what we reckoned would be near impossible. But you did it and I stand corrected! Well done, son . . . well done!"

Then Mr. Schutt handed Edward a splendid uniform with two rows of brass buttons and a grand cap. "I hereby declare you, Edward Pembroke, official Duckmaster of the Peabody Hotel!"

Everyone cheered. Edward's dream had come true. He'd wear that wonderful uniform with the brass buttons and march to John Philip Sousa and be near his beloved ducks.

Over the years Edward Pembroke trained many a duck to march to the fountain in the lobby of the Peabody Hotel in Memphis. He personally trained every one. They served as "Pembroke ducks" for three months or so, then they were returned to the wild—except for John Philip, who stayed for all of his duck life with Edward.

Edward Pembroke served as Duckmaster of the Peabody Hotel for over fifty years. The hotel even named a room after him! When he retired, he moved to his dear little farm just outside of Memphis. There he had his very own pond with John Philip's descendants. But he searched the skies every day, hoping that the wild ducks might land and stay with him too.

But they always flew over and disappeared into the horizon until one day. It was said that on that day, as Edward was sitting by his pond, a John Philip Sousa march came on his radio. He turned it up as loud as it would go, then stood up and doffed his hat. At that very moment, flocks of wild ducks flying overhead rolled out of formation, circled and landed. They marched right up to him and cocked their heads.

They came and came by the hundreds. His graduates all! And for the rest of his days, they say, whenever those ducks passed by, they never failed to stop over and march again with their beloved Duckmaster.

This entirely fictional story of a young man who dared to bring his pet duck to the marbled halls of the famous Peabody Hotel was inspired by the legend of the Peabody Ducks and by the personnel of the Peabody who found a truly original role for the first duck and all of its mates ever since, a role that has lasted for over sixty years.

PATRICIA LEE GAUCH, EDITOR

Copyright © 2004 by Babushka Inc.
All rights reserved. This book, or parts thereof, may not be reproduced in
any form without permission in writing from the publisher,
PHILOMEL BOOKS,
a division of Penguin Young Readers Group,
345 Hudson Street, New York, NY 10014.
Philomel Books, Reg. U.S. Pat. & Tm. Off.
The scanning, uploading and distribution of this book via the Internet or via any other means
without the permission of the publisher is illegal and punishable by law. Please purchase only
authorized electronic editions, and do not participate in or encourage electronic piracy of copy-
righted materials. Your support of the author's rights is appreciated.
Published simultaneously in Canada. Manufactured in China by South China Printing Co. Ltd.
Designed by Semadar Megged. Text set in 16-point Adobe Jenson.
The art was done in watercolor and pencil.
Library of Congress Cataloging-in-Publication Data
Polacco, Patricia. John Philip Duck / Patricia Polacco. p. cm.
Summary: During the Depression, a young Memphis boy trains his pet duck to do tricks in the
fountain of a grand hotel and ends up becoming the Duckmaster of the Peabody Hotel.
[1. Ducks—Fiction. 2. Hotels, motels, etc.—Fiction. 3. Memphis (Tenn.)—Fiction.] I. Title.
PZ7.P75186 Jo 2004 [E]—dc22 2003016987
ISBN 0-399-24262-7
1 2 3 4 5 6 7 8 9 10
First Impression